MARY

The MOTHER of JESUS

✳

TOMIE dePAOLA

Holiday House/New York

For all those I love at Holiday House . . .
Tere, Barbara and especially, Margery, Kate and John.

The Latin from the antiphons in the Benedictine Breviary was translated by Nancy
Worman and adapted by Tomie dePaola. The text regarding Mary's life was retold by
Tomie dePaola, based on legends and biblical accounts. Mr. de Paola referred to *The
New English Bible*, Oxford University Press, Cambridge University Press, 1970, as
his main scriptural source.

Copyright © 1995 by Tomie dePaola
All rights reserved
Printed in the United States of America
Library of Congress Cataloging-in-Publication Data
De Paola, Tomie.
Mary : the mother of Jesus / written and illustrated by Tomie
dePaola.
p.   cm.
ISBN 0-8234-1018-8
1. Mary, Blessed Virgin, Saint — Juvenile literature. [1. Mary,
Blessed Virgin, Saint.   2. Saints.   3. Bible stories — N.T.]
I. Title.
BT607.D4   1995   92-54491   CIP   AC
232.91 — dc20

There is very little in scripture written about Mary, the mother of Jesus. But the legends and myths that surround this holy woman are astounding.

Mary has captured the hearts of people throughout the centuries. Great cathedrals have been built in her honor. Many Christians continue to pray for her intervention. Nearly 80,000 visions of Mary have been claimed since the third century A.D. Only seven have received official recognition by the Catholic church, including six apparitions before three children in Fátima, Portugal in 1917; fourteen-year-old Bernadette Soubirous's eighteen visions in Lourdes, France in 1858; and Mary's appearance to a poor peasant, Juan Diego, in Tepeyac, Mexico in 1531.

When I was an art student in 1956, I saw the Giotto frescoes of the life of Mary in the Arena Chapel in Padua, Italy. I knew that some day, I would attempt my own visual version of Mary's life.

I have drawn on scripture, legend, and tradition for this praise of Mary, the mother of Jesus.

—TdeP
New Hampshire

THE PRESENTATION OF
THE CHILD MARY AT THE TEMPLE

The root of Jesse has produced a sweet stalk, from which has come a flower filled with a wondrous fragrance.

ANTIPHON, THE MAGNIFICAT, II VESPERS,
FEASTS OF SAINTS ANNE AND JOACHIM

There was an old man and an old woman named Joachim and Anne from the royal house of David. God had been good to them except that they were without children. This caused them great sadness.

One evening, while Joachim was away praying in the hills, Anne was walking in the garden. She saw a nest of baby birds and began to cry, because she was childless.

Suddenly an angel appeared to her and said, "Anne, your prayers have been heard. You shall give birth to a daughter who shall be blessed throughout the world." At the same time, an angel appeared to Joachim and told him the same thing.

Anne went out and met her husband at the gate, and they rejoiced together. When her time had come, Anne gave birth to a daughter and her name was called Mary.

When Mary was three years old, her father and mother took her to be presented at the temple. They placed her on the first step, and the little child climbed all the steps to the altar by herself. The high priest received her and kissed her. Blessing her he said, "Mary, the Lord has magnified your name to all generations. In you shall be made known the redemption of all Israel."

And Mary danced with joy, and all of the house of Israel were happy with her and loved her.

THE BETROTHAL OF JOSEPH AND MARY

The just man will flower like a lily.
And he will flourish always before the Lord.

VERSE AND RESPONSE, NONE, FEAST OF SAINT JOSEPH

When Mary became of age, the high priest Zacharias asked the Lord what was to be done concerning her marriage.

An angel appeared to him and said, "Call all the suitors together. Tell each to bring a staff to the temple, and the Lord shall show a sign to one of them. Let him be a husband to Mary."

Now Joseph, the carpenter who was a holy man, brought his staff and left it at the temple, along with the others. The next morning, his staff had blossomed forth into leaves and flowers.

"Joseph," Zacharias said, "you are the one chosen to take Mary from here and keep her for the Lord."

At first, Joseph was afraid, but he took Mary and said to her, "Behold, I have taken you from the temple of the Lord to my house. But I must go and follow my trade of building. I will return, but meanwhile the Lord will watch over you."

So Joseph left and Mary remained in the house.

THE ANNUNCIATION

The angel Gabriel spoke to Mary saying:
"Hail, full of grace; the Lord be with you;
blessed are you among women."

ANTIPHON, THE MAGNIFICAT, II VESPERS, FEAST OF THE ANNUNCIATION

In the sixth month of the year, the angel Gabriel was sent by God to Nazareth with a message for Mary. Entering her house, he said, "Hail. You are full of grace. The Lord is with you." Mary was troubled by this, for she did not know what it meant.

"Don't be afraid, Mary," the angel said, "for God has been gracious to you. You shall conceive and give birth to a son. He shall be called Jesus. He will be known as the Son of the Most High. He will be king over Israel, and his reign will never end!"

"But how can this be?" Mary asked. "I am still a virgin."

The angel said, "The Holy Spirit will come upon you, and the power of the Most High will overshadow you. And the holy child that will be born will be called the Son of God. And behold your cousin Elizabeth has also conceived a son in her old age, because nothing is impossible with God."

And Mary said, "Behold the handmaid of the Lord. As you have spoken, let it be."

And the angel left her.

THE VISITATION

Rising up, Mary went in haste into the mountains, into the land of Judah.

ANTIPHON I, LAUDS, FEAST OF THE VISITATION

Now Joseph found that Mary was with child, and he was very troubled, because they had not come together. Being a kind man he wanted to protect Mary, but at the same time he decided to have the marriage contract set aside. An angel came to Joseph in a dream and said, "Joseph, Son of David, do not be afraid to take Mary as your wife. She is with child by the Holy Spirit. She shall have a son and you shall call him Jesus, because he will save his people from their sins."

Joseph did as the angel said.

Then Mary went into the hill country of Judah to visit her cousin Elizabeth.

Upon hearing Mary's greeting, Elizabeth's baby leapt for joy in her womb.

Elizabeth was filled with the Holy Spirit and said, "Blessed are you among all women and blessed is the fruit of your womb."

And Mary said, "My soul magnifies the Lord, for He that is mighty has done great things to me and Holy is His name."

THE BIRTH OF JESUS

The Word was made flesh. Alleluia, Alleluia.
And it has dwelt in us. Alleluia.

VERSE AND RESPONSE, LAUDS, CHRISTMAS DAY

In those days, a decree was issued by the Emperor Augustus that all must be counted in their own town. So Joseph and Mary, who was great with child, went from Nazareth to Bethlehem because Joseph was of the house of David.

When they got there, Mary gave birth to her firstborn son and wrapped him in swaddling clothes. She laid him in a manger because there was no room in the inn.

In fields nearby were certain shepherds watching over their flocks by night, when suddenly an angel of the Lord appeared to them and said, "Fear not. For I bring good tidings of great joy. For tonight in the town of Bethlehem a Savior is born who is Christ, the Lord. You will find him wrapped in swaddling clothes and lying in a manger."

All at once there was with the angel a multitude of heavenly hosts singing and praising, "Glory to God in the highest and on earth, peace to men of goodwill."

"Let us go and see this thing that has come to pass," the shepherds said to each other. And they did.

THE PRESENTATION OF THE BOY JESUS IN THE TEMPLE

This day the blessed virgin Mary presented the boy Jesus in the temple.

ANTIPHON, THE MAGNIFICAT, II VESPERS,
FEAST OF THE PURIFICATION OF THE BLESSED VIRGIN MARY

Eight days later, after the purification rites were completed, Joseph and Mary brought the baby Jesus to the temple in Jerusalem. They had with them two turtledoves as an offering according to the law of Moses.

There was at that time in Jerusalem a holy man called Simeon. God had promised that he would not die until he had seen the Messiah. When Joseph and Mary brought in the baby Jesus, Simeon took him in his arms and praised God, saying, "This day, O Lord, your promise is fulfilled, for my eyes have seen your salvation which you have prepared for all people."

Joseph and Mary were full of wonder. Simeon blessed them and said to Mary, "This child is destined to be rejected by men and your heart too shall be pierced."

THE ADORATION OF THE MAGI

Like a flame of fire, that star pointed out God.

ANTIPHON 4, I VESPERS, EPIPHANY

After the birth of Jesus, there came from the East three wise men. They arrived in Jerusalem at the court of King Herod, asking, "Where is he that has been born King of the Jews, for we have seen his star and have come to pay him homage." Herod was greatly disturbed. He was the king and wanted no other to take his place.

He called the wise men to him. "When you find this king, come back and tell me, so I may worship him too." But Herod wanted to harm the baby king.

When the wise men went out from King Herod's court, the star appeared again and went ahead of them until it stopped at the place where the child was with his mother Mary. Entering into the house, they bowed to the ground. Then they opened their treasures of gold, frankincense, and myrrh.

And being warned in a dream not to go back to Herod, they returned home another way.

THE FLIGHT INTO EGYPT

A voice was heard in Rama, moaning and wailing,
Rachel weeping for her children.

ANTIPHON 4, LAUDS, FEAST OF THE HOLY INNOCENTS

After the wise men had gone, an angel appeared in a dream to Joseph. "Take the child and his mother from here and escape with them into Egypt," the angel said. "Stay there until I tell you, for Herod is going to search for the child to do away with him."

So Joseph took Mary and Jesus away into Egypt.

Now, Herod found out that the wise men had tricked him and had gone home by another way. He fell into a rage and ordered that all children up to two years old be slaughtered in Bethlehem and its neighborhood.

The time came when Herod died. An angel appeared again to Joseph in Egypt and said, "Rise up. Take the child and his mother and go with them to the land of Israel, for the men that would harm the child are dead!"

Joseph took Mary and the child Jesus and went to the region of Galilee and they settled in Nazareth.

THE BOY JESUS IN THE TEMPLE

When they were returning, the boy Jesus stayed in Jerusalem and his parents did not know it.

ANTIPHON 2, LAUDS, FEAST OF SAINT JOSEPH

It was the custom for Joseph and Mary to go every year to Jerusalem for the feast of Passover. The boy Jesus was twelve, and they made the journey as always. When the festival time was over, they started for home. The boy Jesus, however, stayed in Jerusalem. Mary and Joseph did not know this, as they were with a great company of people. They had traveled for a whole day before they realized that Jesus was not with them.

They returned to Jerusalem and searched for him. After three days, Mary and Joseph found the boy Jesus sitting in the temple among the teachers, listening to them and asking and answering questions. All who heard him were astonished at his wisdom and the answers he gave.

His parents were surprised to find him at the temple. Mary said to him, "My son, why have you done this? Your father and I have been searching for you, with great worry!"

"Why did you search?" Jesus said. "Didn't you know I was in my Father's house?"

Mary and Joseph did not understand what he meant.

Jesus went back to Nazareth with them and remained in their care. And Mary kept all these things in her heart.

THE MARRIAGE AT CANA

A marriage was held in Cana in Galilee and Jesus was there with his mother Mary.

ANTIPHON, THE BENEDICTUS, LAUDS, 2ND SUNDAY AFTER EPIPHANY

Shortly after Jesus was baptized by John, there was a marriage at Cana in Galilee. Mary, the mother of Jesus, was there, and Jesus and some of his disciples were also guests. The wine ran out, so Mary went to Jesus and said, "They have no more wine." And Jesus answered, "What is that to me, Mother? My hour has not come yet."

Mary went to the servants and said, "Do whatever he tells you." There were six stone water jars standing near. "Fill these jars with water," Jesus said, and the servants filled them to the brim. "Now draw off some and take it to the head steward," Jesus ordered, and the servants did. The steward tasted the water now turned into wine, not knowing where it came from, although the servants knew.

The steward went to the bridegroom. "Everyone serves the best wine first," he said, "and after the guests have drunk freely, they serve the poorer wine, but you have kept the best wine until now."

This was the first miracle of Jesus.

THE MINISTRY

Each and every day, I shall praise you, O Lord.

ANTIPHON 3, FRIDAY VESPERS

Jesus' ministry lasted three years. He performed many miracles and healed many people. He brought a new law to the people, and some say that Mary was always with the disciples and the women who followed Jesus on his travels.

MARY'S SOLITUDE

Sorrow has oppressed me, and my face has swelled with weeping, and my eyelashes have become darkly misted.

ANTIPHON, THE MAGNIFICAT, II VESPERS,
FEAST OF THE SEVEN SORROWS OF THE BLESSED VIRGIN MARY

When Jesus was led out to be crucified, the women followed as he carried his cross through the streets. Mary, his mother, was among them. The soldiers nailed him to the cross. Mary stood near with Mary, wife of Clopas, Mary of Magdala, and the disciple John.

Jesus saw her with John and said to her, "Mother, there is your son." Then he said to John, "There is your mother," and from that moment John took Mary into his own home.

At the third hour when Jesus died, his body was taken from the cross and Mary held her son for the last time.

The words of Simeon all those years ago had come true, as a sword seemed to pass through her heart.

THE COMING OF THE HOLY SPIRIT

*The Spirit of the Lord has filled
the circle of the lands. Alleluia.*

ANTIPHON 2, I VESPERS, FEAST OF PENTECOST

For forty days, after his resurrection from the dead, Jesus walked with his disciples. On the fortieth day, while on Mount Olivet, he rose into heaven but promised them all that the Holy Spirit would come to them.

They returned to Jerusalem and went to the room upstairs where they were staying. Mary, the mother of Jesus, was with them. There were many people present, and they prayed together. Suddenly a noise came from the sky like that of a strong wind, and it filled the whole house. Then there appeared tongues of fire that separated and rested on each of them. And they were all filled with the Holy Spirit.

MARY IS TAKEN TO HEAVEN

Mary has been taken up into heaven:
the Angels rejoice, praising, they bless the Lord.

ANTIPHON 1, 1 VESPERS, FEAST OF THE ASSUMPTION

In the small house of the Last Supper, Mary lay on the narrow bed, surrounded by the disciples who had come to see her. She lay dying. But she was not sad or afraid — only waiting for the moment when she would be again with her beloved son. Her death was so gentle it was as if she fell asleep. Mary the mother of Jesus was wrapped in the linen shroud and placed in the tomb. And like her son's tomb, a large stone was rolled across the entrance.

The apostle Thomas arrived when it was too late. An angel appeared to him and said, "Come. Push the stone aside." Thomas did, and there was the empty winding sheet, dazzling white. Mary had been taken up to heaven, body and soul, to sit on the throne next to her Divine Son.

THE QUEEN OF HEAVEN

*A great sign has appeared in the heavens: A woman
cloaked in the sun, and the moon under her feet, and
on her head a crown of twelve stars.*

CHAPTER AT NONE, REVELATION 12, 1,
FEAST OF THE IMMACULATE CONCEPTION